When We Become Giants

First Edition

Reddig, Jeremy

When We Become Giants: *A Tale From The Forces We all Experience* / Jeremy Reddig. – 1ˢᵗ ed.

Library of Congress Control Number: 2019904853

eBook: 978-0-9969561-3-0
Paperback: 978-0-9969561-2-3

Printed in the United States of America

1. Fiction (visionary and metaphysical) 2. Fiction (psychological)

3. Philopsychonomics (philosophy, psychology, economics)

1 2 3 5 8 13 21 34 55 89 144

Published by Mobiusynergy PO Box 182782 Arlington, TX. 76096

When We Become Giants

A Tale From The Forces We all Experience

Jeremy Reddig

When We Become Giants is dedicated to those who wish to be of service for all as we thrive toward universal sustainment. Let this story help you achieve your wildest dreams.

You know those dreams you have that only you believe in?

Those dreams are your vision of what is possible. These visions are based on your unique outlook on life.

For the sake of humanity, please believe in and choose your vision when possible. Said dreams might be the only thing that will help the Universe thrive.

For we are all on earth together, and somewhere out there is a tribe waiting to help bring your vision to life.

WHEN WE BECOME GIANTS

SPECIAL THANKS TO

Thanks Dean Lindsey, for being my mentor over at the National Speakers Association North Texas chapter, and for encouraging me to THRIVE!

Thanks Madison Durapau and the Tarrant County College editing department for teaching me how to become a better writer while helping me enhance this story.

If you ever see Wilder Jones, thank him for verifying certain parts of the story to ensure quality.

I would also like to thank Daniel Baumgartner, Marylee Mims, and Karyn Smith for all their help over at Toastmasters.

And well I am at it. I want to thank my family and friends who never stop believing in me and pushing me to THRIVE toward my dreams.

$$= + = + =$$

Imagine you are looking into one of those one-way mirror's people use when observing an experiment or interrogating suspects of a crime. In this case we are attempting to figure out a way that can help us unleash the human minds' potential.

There are two people; Mauli, who we hired; and Slobodan, our guinea pig.

We see both in this all white laboratory with a pillar in the center of the room and on it sits a shiny red lever.

PERFECT: This should be enough background information to get this show on the road. Afterall, I do not want to be the one that ruins the tale for you, so please journey onward at your leisure.

ONCE UPON A LEVER

Imagine the sound of a fire alarm going off as we activate the sirens right now.

Bweep Bweep Bweep…

Mauli Kamali starts off by saying, "I don't have a good feeling about this."

Slobodan looks at the lever that we placed in the middle of the room.

While at the same time, Mauli cautiously points at the lever and continues, "Slobodan, nothing good ever comes from pulling that lever."

Bweep Bweep Bweep…

Slobodan Kuuipo's entire body froze. "What do you suppose we do?"

Mauli knows how powerful you are and is not ready to let you or this study down.

Mauli puts on an act and begins pacing back and forth and begins breathing faster to create a sense of urgency. "We need to do something or else we are both finished, and this work would have been a waste of energy!"

Slobodan contemplates for a few more seconds before saying, "I got this."

Bweep Bweep Bweep…

Mauli was quick to respond, "Slobodan wait, think this through. Pulling the lever is a slippery…"

But, by the time Mauli could finish. Slobodan sprung out of that frozen state to pull the lever like they were ready to blast off into space at the speed of light. "Done!" yelled Slobodan. The sirens immediately went silent and a ginormous amount of energy started spiraling out of thin air to activate a galaxy looking type of a portal.

Mauli continues by saying, "…slope that will lead to a path you might not want to go down!" Mauli pats Slobodan on the back, and confidently says while death staring straight into Slobodan's eyes. "Welp, I guess we are on the same team now… Hakuna matata Slobodan, I was born to protect us."

ACTIVATE THE FORCE FIELD

Slobodan yells, "dude!" While turning toward the exit to look at Mauli. "Relax, everything will be okay, it always works out." Slobodan thinks to self, my *mind is powerful, we'll manage.*

Mauli knew they were both in for a surprise but didn't have any clue as to what was beyond this portal, "Yea; keep telling yourself everything will be alright." Then Mauli thinks, *I sure hope Slobodan is the one*; before saying out loud, "Try not to make all of your decisions that fast, we don't exactly know what we are up against."

Slobodan gets ready to throw up his air quotes. "your 'bad feeling' doesn't make my action wrong."

Mauli's head begins shaking, "think Slow… bo… dan." *Powerful mind my ass,* Mauli thought. Just before saying, "this isn't just about you anymore; hopefully we get out of this situation alive."

Slobodan cheerfully shrugged his shoulders and with confidence says, "no worries, as the saying goes, 'we dug our graves, now we have to sleep in them.'"

Mauli paid no attention to Slobodan's naïve remark and pointed to the portal "Sure looks fantastically vibrant."

Slobodan jokingly said, "No shit captain obvious, it's a portal, all portals look out of this world. Let's go."

Mauli was looking into the portal to see if they could see what was on the other side. "Slobodan, you have no idea what you just got us into. This is no ordinary portal."

Slobodan takes a breath while standing up straight to correct his posture before looking at Mauli. "Till the end."

Mauli responds, "Till the end," as they both go in for a fist bump.

INTO THE WONDERLAND

Mauli gets closer to the portal "When we crossover..."

Slobodan moves toward Mauli's side and interrupts, "I guess it's now or never," jumping into the portal; leaving Mauli in the laboratory mid-sentence.

Mauli looks at us on the other side of the one-way mirror. "...Why!?" Turns back around a mutters "what did I get myself into accepting this job?"

Mauli looks back at the portal, takes a breath and jumps into catch up to Slobodan. The portal closes, and we are left wondering where they went in hopes that they find what we need and return with a message.

In a split second Mauli gets to the other side and immediately asks Slobodan, "Are you in a hurry or something?"

Slobodan is walking over to a ball of energy where he sits down before responding. "Why are you asking if I am in a hurry? I just couldn't wait to jump into a portal" Slobodan thinks, *it is something I have always wanted to do.* Slobodan looks at Mauli standing taller than the apple tree and points. "Look, we must be 33 feet taller after going through the portal."

Mauli bends over to pick an apple from the crown of the tree, and thinks, *I guess this is what it feels like to be a giant.* "We are… GIANTS, pretty cool." Tossing the apple into the air, Mauli's mouth opens to catch it like people typically do with a grape. *Chomp, crisp, crunch, gulp…*

Meanwhile, Slobodan attempts to comprehend the world around him; *herons hovering in the heavens; hares hopping through fields of hemp; bees with bellies full of honey; and hungry hippos humping in the hydro hills.*

Slobodan asks the million-dollar question, "Mauli, where are we?"

As Mauli picks a couple of apples to store in the satchel. "Our graves, and now we have to sleep in them."

Slobodan begins to wonder if *Mauli is out of his mind* and asks again, "Mauli… where are we?"

WE REAP WHAT WE CHOOSE

Slobodan stood up from the ball of energy. "Dude. If you're trying to blow my mind it isn't working, where are we, is this a suicide mission or something, I want to go home!?"

Mauli closes the satchel, and takes a few steps back to face Slobodan and says, "I tried to tell you about this experience before you jumped in. Now you have no choice but to help,"

You must help, Mauli thought.

Slobodan quietly yells within, *Help!? Haven't I been helping?* "Enlighten me Mauli, what do you need me to do?" Slobodan backs up to the ball of energy and plops down on it awaiting Mauli's response.

Mauli back pedals in hopes that Slobodan will relax before answering the question. "We need you to develop a creative solution that will help the peoples' minds as they have been working tirelessly to overcome their stress, anxiety, and depression. No matter how hard they try to make their lives better they can't seem to stop spiraling out of control; Earth is in turmoil Slobodan, and the people need leaders like you who can lead by example to help them thrive."

Mauli takes a few steps toward Slobodan to make this point as clear as possible. "Your actions brought us to a creative experience. This place is your ideal imaginary world approximately 100 years in the future, a black hole if you will … energy within, energy between ... [they both look around at all of the energy between them as they naturally feel their energy within] Slobodan, you are the only one that can get us out of this situation, and I'm with you till the end," Mauli's fist extends for a fist bump.

Slobodan laughs in astonishment and thinks, *what did I get myself into this time?* "Get your hand out of here [slapping Mauli's hand out of the way], you mean to tell me that I am the only one who can get us out of this 'creative experience,'

And!

For us to get out of here we have to develop a solution to help the psychological warfare that has been going on for god… who knows how long?"

Mauli thought, *you're confused, I get it,* "You chose yourself when you decided to pull the lever, and being that this is your virtual world, only you can get us out."

IN SEARCH OF A CREATIVE SOLUTION

There is a puzzling look on Slobodan's face, *I brought us here?* "Mauli, how did I bring us here? You were the one that brought me into the laboratory."

Mauli looks down and kicks the tiny pebbles forming the many paths they can take on their journey ahead. "Great question Slobodan, for starters, you pulled the lever… Not only did you pull the lever, but you jumped in, and left me no choice but to follow."

Slobodan jumps up from the ball of energy and thinks aloud, "Wait a minute, you brought me to the laboratory with one lever in the middle and told me that we have to figure out how to help our minds while sustaining the human collective with a creative solution. The alarm went off, and next thing I know the lever was pulled."

Mauli interrupts, "which you pulled."

Slobodan looks at Mauli as if this was a known fact between them, "the lever was pulled, I get that Mauli, the portal opened, and then we jumped in."

Mauli's head starts shaking side-to-side before saying, "you jumped in, and I followed… capeesh?"

Slobodan asks for clarification purposes, "So, you're telling me it's my fault we are here?

[pausing to think for a second]

I should have discussed the situation with you." While accepting the cold hard facts Slododan thought, *shoulda woulda coulda.*

Mauli smirks as a sign of relief while thinking, *I'm glad you didn't ask me anything, or else I'd be stuck looking for someone else to pull the damn lever.* "Yes Slobodan, you brought us here. Now that you understand let's be on our way, so we can get back to our loved ones."

They both start walking down one of the pebbled paths that has a sign that reads 'this way to the Hydro Hills.

Slobodan's stomach makes a sound; bawr-buh-rig-mahy …

Mauli reaches into the satchel to grab an apple, "Catch," and tosses it into the air for Slobodan to catch.

Slobodan catches and holds on to the apple as they begin walking down the path looking around at the clear blue sky, vibrant landscape, and a pond that is coming up on their right. As they approach the pond Mauli decides to take this moment to provide a better sense of understanding, "Believe it or not, out of all the potential candidates you were the only one that pulled the lever. Everyone else pushed the button to open the door. They left the room, and I was stuck looking for someone who would pull the lever on their own."

Slobodan thought, *why didn't I think about,* "The button to open the door? I didn't see a button."

Mauli takes a breath, "yes the button, after I said, 'I have a bad feeling about this.' The others always asked me 'what was going on with my feelings' I told them they can either push the button to get out of here or pull the lever to go into their ideal world to work on a solution to help sustain the human collective. A classic red pill, blue pill situation with a twist." Mauli's hands move in a way that is revealing the world around them. "and this my friend, is your wonderland."

Slobodan contemplates and says, "No one else pulled the…"

Mauli interrupts, "No, no one else pulled the lever. You were the only one that didn't even ask what was going on. You simply led the way…

Blindly if I may add."

Slobodan thinks, *I'm such an idiot.* "I guess this is my calling," tossing the apple into the air to eat, *chomp, crisp, crunch ... gulp.*

ABSORB THE WORLD AROUND

"Mauli, if I am the only one who pulled the lever, what is the problem that we need to solve?"

Mauli looks at Slobodan and then back to the trail ahead. "I was wondering how long it would take you to ask. In this harmonized world of yours there isn't a problem."

They continue walking side-by-side absorbing the cohesive world around them and the animals flowing in their natural habitat. They feel the wind that is vigorously strengthening the stems of the plants and branches on the trees, the mist that is quenching thirsty organisms. And, up in the sky sits a ginormous shining star that is beaming down on them with rays of might. Slobodan thinks, *this star must be bigger than the Earth's Sun.*

Mauli continues, "Slobodan, this world presents an opportunity for us to observe a reality where you can figure out what is being done right." Mauli took a few breaths and after careful consideration said, "Can you feel the peaceful environment around you?"

Slobodan's eyes close for a second to feel the world they are in. "Yes, I do, and it smells fantastically fresh, *this air smells better than back in the city.*"

Mauli replies, "Exactly my thought. Your senses are peacefully present and there isn't much in the way of conflict right about now."

Slobodan took a deep breath, *ah, so relaxing, I can stay here for a while;* "wait a minute, how and the hell are we going to get out of here?"

Mauli said, "By going deeper Slobodan, we are within energy, between energy; but you need to go deeper to understand what this phrase means." Mauli looks at Slobodan's expressionless stare off into space. *I don't know how else to say it,* Mauli said, "You need to figure out what is happening that is allowing this world to remain in a peaceful state."

Slobodan thinks, *oh, that's it?*, and asks to clarify their purpose here; "All you need me to do is to figure out what is going on, so we can implement the solution back home to help people cope with their life experiences?"

Mauli's head nods up and down. "Yup. That's it, then we are on our merry way."

As they are coming up to the pond, Slobodan replies with excitement, "okay, let's get this done so we can get out of here… [pointing at the pond] Look it's a bird with one foot in the water and the other on land." Slobodan thought while walking toward the bird with long toes, *I'm going to see what this is all about,* "Hey bird can you talk?" The Heron responded "No." Slobodan reached over and hit Mauli in the chest out of pure amazement. "Did you hear that Mauli!? Tell me you heard that!?"

Mauli responds, "Yes. Apparently, the animals talk around here."

Slobodan does a little dance move to express a sense of accomplishment. "Finally, we are getting somewhere." Slobodan looks back at the Heron and asks, "why do you have one foot in water and the other on grass?"

The Heron boisterously said, "Energy within, energy between"

Slobodan hung his head in shame, "Great! Back to square one …"

EVERYTHING YOU NEED IS WITHIN

The Heron responds with a sense of sarcasm, "easy pet, I'll transform your life if you let me... I am present and patiently waiting within energy, between energy." The Heron moves his head, and wings, but his legs and feet remain unwavering. "You see pet, we are all seeking an experience, and we must be prepared when the opportunity presents itself or else, we won't be able to grab life by the cojones."

Slobodan thinks, *this bird keeps calling me a pet.* Then says, "we are trying to find out what makes 'energy within, energy between' a harmonious experience for all.

What makes you harmoniously intertwined with this world?"

The Heron looked at Slobodan, blinks three times and says, "I am neither here nor there, and I am presently within and between all of this energy we come to experience. I am within myself, and I am myself. I am not trying to be you, and I don't expect you to be me. We are all different and we must express our individuality in a way that works for us. When this happens, you'll understand yourself and the strengths and opportunities you ought to be preparing yourself for."

Slobodan thought out loud, "So we have to focus on within to find out how we can live a life that works for us?"

The Heron confirms, "Correct, everything you need is within. Once you understand who you are within. You will be able to truly work with and help people when the right opportunities arise.

When you understand who you are, and how you operate. The ability to peacefully conquer your life and help others do the same effectively increases. To do this pet, you must understand that we all have thoughts and feelings that come from within. Our lives will attract, demand, and manifest chaos when we don't make the connection with the energy between. Simply because we cannot establish a relationship with the force."

Slobodan was processing what he just heard. *A peaceful conquest ... the force? I guess conquering myself is better than someone else conquering me.* Slobodan notices that the Herons legs have been as still as the statue of liberty. "What are you waiting for?"

The Heron looks at the Giants. "I'm sunbathing." Then looks down and moves his beak toward the water. When suddenly, the Heron stabs the water with his beak to catch a fish. He immediately launches off the ground to take flight. While soaring toward the heavens the Heron grabs the fish with his claws and yells, "GO FIND THE BEES!"

Slobodan turns to Mauli and says, "the Heron was calling us pets right?"

Mauli bursts out laughing, "No my friend, he was calling you the pet. He never once said pets. Now, now, let's go find these bees he was talking about. Maybe they will have some honey to share with us."

FOCUS ON THE PATH AHEAD

As the two-start walking Slobodan looks up at the Heron flying away and says, "Mauli … I like what the Heron was saying, and I can see how most people back home aren't within their energy, or between their energy as most believe they are always without the abundant resources that are always available to them."

Mauli asked, "Why is that?"

Slobodan responded, "Because the masses are distracted by things that are beyond their control and on top of that, being selfish is viewed as a bad thing. It's backward because we must take care of ourselves before we can help others. You saw the Heron, he provided wisdom to us while snagging that fish to eat; it's a natural phenomenon. The Heron needs to refuel his energy levels to maintain optimal health.

For all we know, the Heron was taking the fish to some other species that needs to eat but are terrible at hunting. Kind of like how parents go off to work to put food on the table and a roof over their kids' heads. All the while, the kids learn about who they are and what they want to accomplish in life."

As they continue walking down the path in search for the bees, Mauli says, "You might be onto something pet, keep a lookout for some beehives, hopefully, we will see some down by the hemp fields."

Slobodan says, "Stop! Don't call me a pet, I am not your pet."

Mauli smiles, and happily responds. "You are not, but I wanted to see when you'd finally speak up and say something."

Slobodan thought, *speak up? I was respecting the Heron, so he would help us.* Slobodan pointed at a tiny spec of energy buzzing past them, "Mauli look! a bee!"

Mauli looks at the bee. "Good eye Slobodan! Let's follow it to the hive."

WE CAN USE YOUR HELP

Mauli and Slobodan follow the bee and began to see more bees as they get closer to the hive.

Mauli wondered, *how are we going to talk to The Queen bee?*

Slobodan wondered, *will the hive welcome us with open wings*?

And as they both turned the corner, at the same time they said, "holy hive!" As if this was a known title for an 11-story hive.

Slobodan continues, "This is the biggest hive I have ever seen in my life. It's like they made this hive specifically for us to walk in and talk to The Queen herself."

Mauli's jaw was dropping lower and lower.

Slobodan notices that they can potentially walk right in. "Seriously, we are giants, but we are small compared to this thing, if it hadn't been for the mountains, we could have seen this from the portal when we entered."

As they approach the hive with caution, one of the warrior bees flew out of the hive and up to about eye height with the giants and said, "Who sent you?"

Slobodan's stands straight up, shoulders back and down, and says, "The Heron told us to go find the bees."

The warrior bee buzzes around for a few seconds while starring both giants directly in their eyes, and says, "I'll be right back," and flew off into the hive.

Mauli says, "he must be communicating to the rest that we are here."

Suddenly both Giants here the sound of a bunch of bees moving.

Bzzzz, bzzzz, bzzzzz …

Mauli thinks, *oh no, they are about to swarm.* The first fleet of bees came rushing out of the hive and flew around Mauli, and Slobodan in a perfect figure eight path. During this time the Bees fly at full speed spreading out across their path to form a glowing infinity sign in broad daylight with both Giants in the center of each loop; an experience these Giants will never forget as they were terrified of being stung to death. One after another the bees kept buzzing around these two Giants. Neither of them moved a muscle as they didn't want to get stung. Finally, after the area was secure, one of the faster bees flew into the hive to inform the Queen.

She then gave the signal for the usher bees to carry her out to the Giants. The usher bees march the Queen's carrier out of the entry way of the Hive to meet with the Giants.

As the Queen is carried out of the hive and she sees the Giants she says in a commanding voice, "My, you are both really tall. I'm not sure where you came from, but today is your lucky day, I only came out for the Heron. We sort of have a working relationship, if you know what I mean?"

Slobodan responds "No, I don't know what you mean, but we are honored that you are taking the time to speak with us…

We can use your help."

The Queen vibrates and says, "Help, with what?" She thinks, *haven't we been helping?*

Slobodan gets straight to the point. "We need help figuring out why energy within, energy between is so important for the mind. So far, I can see that it is important because we spiritually transcend as we thrive toward sustaining the universe."

The Queen looked back at some of the usher bees, whispering a command. She turned back to Mauli and Slobodan, "I see, you came to ask about the Honey…."

Huh, Slobodan had that confused look. "No, not exactly, we are looking for solutions to improve our current state back home … but if you are about to drop some knowledge on us as to why honey has something to do with energy within, energy between, please …

Don't let me or this Giant (pointing to Mauli) stop you."

The Queen starts heading back into the Hive. "Well then, this way."

Mauli and Slobodan follow the usher bees who were carrying the Queen back inside.

THERE IS SO MUCH YOU CAN DO

The Giants were escorted into the Queens comb of command. Where they could see the entire operation in all its wax and honey. Mauli continues the conversation by saying, "thank you for inviting us in, we have never had the pleasure of being in a hive before."

The Queen relaxes in her carriage as she is flown up to her throne. "you are welcome, just don't expect to distract my tribe, they are busy working together for the betterment of our environment."

"Environment?" Slobodan asked.

The Queen looks around the hive and says, "Yes, from the beginning of our little bee lives we have been a major key to the survival of plants. We help the plants spread across the universe, so we can also be attributed to helping human civilization as those plants and trees bare food for you all to eat."

She continues, "like humans, we work ourselves to death, but there is a difference."

Slobodan interrupts, "what's that your Highness?"

The Queen continues, "We work for the good of the colony based on our abilities. Whereas, some humans are distracted by all the marvels to the point of having no idea what they truly want out of life, and as a result they build not for the collective, but for someone else's dreams. Some humans work to make someone else happy instead of making themselves happy by doing what they are interested in."

Slobodan asks, "what if someone else's dreams are for the betterment of the collective?"

The Queen was quick to respond, "that would be fantastic, but often dreams aren't for the betterment, because of the intolerable differences that force humans into situations they don't fully understand. You must go beyond surviving and working to put food on the table, we bees and the rest of the non-human ecosystem are doing that work for you.

And trust me when I say, 'we aren't doing it for the money.' These are simply our actions in the Universal Tribe allowing all energy within the universe to unite as a cohesive tribe of tribes."

Slobodan thinks, *beyond survival* and asks, "what do you mean, beyond survival?"

The Queen walks toward the edge where she can stare off into the hive to see many of the bees working. "Look, the bees are working their asses off for true sociality to co-exist and support each other for the Hive. As a result, they pollinate the land, and as a by-product, they bring nectar and pollen back to the hive that we turn into honey … these actions are all a part of our spiritual transformation …

Slobodan, the world is an ecosystem, and we aren't the only ones helping in a manner that keeps life alive and well. The world depends on us, and we depend on the world. Just like the fields of hemp, the hares, the heron, the apple trees and all the other species that have evolved up and to this point. In addition to these dependents, we even count on the humans to keep us alive.

We are all one; energy within, energy between. We all experience from within, yet we are all between as we share and create a better world that is always working with us rather than against us."

Slobodan thinks, *I never thought the bees were working so hard to keep us alive;* and says, "Between the universes situations and within ourselves… so how do we move beyond survival?"

The Queen commands, "Stop hurting yourselves! In turn, you are hurting us. Figure out what works for you on an individual level, and how you can use those skills to work with a tribe toward the common goal: sustainability of life through true sociality. Figure out how society can nurture not just your kids, but all the kids. Afterall, we are all kids to someone aren't we?

Allow the kids to divide themselves based on their abilities; not on what society wants them to be, but on what they are willing and able to become. Because that my friend is inspiring, and inspiration radiates positive energy that is contagious. Once you can sustain the collective, the collective will begin to thrive. The hive does the same thing every single day and each bee knows what must be done to keep perpetuating abundance and prosperity. Bee's only live for a short amount of time, so we are continuously learning, working, playing, and morphing into a sustaining spiritual force of positive energy that reproduces and encourages life."

The Giants and the Queen sit in silence as they listen to the bees doing work for the Universal Tribe.

Bzzzz, bzzzz, bzzzzz …

Then the Queen continues, "I must admit, we do our job pretty well. Our network spans virtually everywhere. We are on every continent, and in the minds of most experiential beings as they either love us, or fear that we will sting them to death. The only thing we aren't a fan of are all of the toxic parasites and pesticides … it's our kryptonite."

Slobodan and Mauli look at each other as if they both simultaneously had the thought, *parasites and pesticides*. Slobodan looks around, and then locks eyes with The Queen, "I wish there was something we can do?"

The Queen batted her wings out of pure inspiration, "There is so much you can do! We are only bee's and look at what we have accomplished; you are humans and have capabilities beyond most species. You just let the negative emotions get the best of each other. Figure out how to co-exist, and you will not only empower the Human Tribe, but will in turn empower the life force that sustains the universe." She claps her legs together, which you can say is code for the hive to bring some of her special honey she calls Thriven Honey.

Slobodan continues, "Well, that was nice of you to say. Sometimes it takes someone else seeing a certain level of ability within another and helping them to nurture that ability for great things to happen."

SYNERGIZE THE CONNECTIONS IN LIFE

The Thriven Honey shows up and The Queen says, "I would like for the both of you to try some Thriven Honey, its medicinal and you will find a great deal of benefits... tell me, Giant, have I helped you at all with the whole "energy within, energy between" situation?"

I think so, Slobodan pondered before saying, "Yes your Highness."

Slobodan and Mauli start walking over to the Thriven Honey and stick their hands into the barrel to scoop up a hand full of honey; they start licking it off their hands like a giant spoon full of peanut butter.

Slobodan continues, "the people back home need help realizing the energy within, and the energy between. With this energy comes a vast amount of personal power like the Heron, and the responsibility to contribute greatly to society like the Hive and for all who are fortunate enough to experience life."

Slobodan looks around to absorb how focused the Bees are on their work being done to sustain life. Noticing some honey was about to drip when Slobodan quickly connects tongue-to-hand to catch the sweet nectar straight from the Queen's private reserve. "Truly magical your highness, with this power we can work on sustaining our minds, so we can then thrive as a collective. Isn't that right Mauli!?"

Slobodan, and The Queen look at Mauli; who gives a thumb up while devouring the honey.

I'll take that as a yes, Slobodan thought.

The Queen was satisfied, as she knew that energy used in such a way to sustain the human existence would in turn, sustain the Hives existence.

The Queen says, "I'm glad you enjoy the honey. It comes from the fields of hemp, lavender, and other surrounding resources." She yawns then continues, "today flew by, it is getting late, you both must be exhausted. You'll rest here for the night."

She commands the nursing bees to prep the bees wax rooms for their guest to rest when ready. "I must excuse myself. When the both of you are ready the nurses will show you the way."

Slobodan realized The Queen was getting ready to leave and said, "thanks for all your help, you really helped clear up our situation back home and we are forever indebted to you and the Heron."

The Queen was already on her way as she paused and said, "Just be sure to do your part, or else it would have been a waste of everyone's energy," and carried on in the direction she was headed. *"See you tomorrow!"* Slobodan boisterously stated as The Queen disappeared into one of the combs.

Mauli looks at Slobodan, "Slobodan, I want to thank you for going on this journey. We have been waiting a long time for someone to qualify themselves, and you did. Thanks, it was an honor to be on your team, and I look forward to working with you when we get back."

All Slobodan heard was get back and repeats, "Back?"

Mauli's head nods up and down. "Yes, you should be able to figure out how to get us back, now that we have The Queen s approval."

Slobodan looks around for a lever but doesn't see anything that looks like a portal activator. "How do we get back?"

Mauli says, "Let's not concern ourselves with that now. We have been on this journey non-stop since we started. Let's get some rest so we can have all of the energy we need to get back."

Slobodan anxiously said, "Nurses, please assist us to our rooms, we have a big day ahead of us!"

The nurse bees guide them to the rooms within the Holy Hive where they would lay to rest.

The two giants lay down in their beds. Mauli says, "sweet dreams."

Slobodan says, "goodnight." They both had so much honey in their bellies they went right to sleep.

FORCEFULLY PULL YOURSELF OUT

When the sun came glaring through their window, they immediately woke up.

Slobodan happily said, "Good morning, time to get up. We have a big day ahead of us"

Mauli stretches and yawns, "Good morning, today is a big day indeed. Once we figure out how to get out of here, we will be on our way back where you can deliver the message to the powerful people who paid for this experiment."

Slobodan gets up from the bed and walks to the window to look for a clue, "Whoa! Mauli come check this out, it is a lake of honey." Mauli springs out of bed and hastily drifts to the window to see this lake. Not only do they both see this lake, but they notice a huge piece of plastic tubing that is spitting out honey at the bottom. Following the slide up to their room, they notice a bee's wax door. Slobodan opens the door to see what was behind but did so in a way that allows Mauli to see what was inside first. Mauli sees other doors, and they both heard a sound of raging honey shooting down a tube like a massive water slide. They walk in and Slobodan said, "let's shoot down this slide swim around for a bit then head back in to see The Queen before we leave."

Mauli's secures a power pose, "are you asking me or telling me?"

Slobodan moves closer to the slide, "Both … come on it will be fun, and obviously this is an appropriate thing to do or else it wouldn't be connected to the room The Queen put us in."

Mauli is silent for a second …, "Okay, let's do it."

Slobodan takes a step back to let Mauli pass, "Perfect, you go first, and I'll be right behind you."

Mauli wastes no time launching down the tube; kind of like a track runner exploding off the line of a 100-meter race. Slobodan followed. They were both screaming and shouting just like kids do when they are having the time of their life.

Mauli shoots out the tube and into the lake. Then Slobodan launches out, breaking the surface of the lake.

Unknowingly, Slobodan enters this deep conscious state of meditation. Slobodan's eyes were wide open, but there was nothing to see. With this feeling of falling into the lake of honey Slobodan begins to see this glowing ring in a pitch-black space and screams, *is anyone out there,* but no one can hear, not even Mauli.

Slobodan begins to float to the top. When a sound is made.

Ding.

Slobodan thought, *what now? That ding sounded like an elevator, but I'm in a lake of honey. Where could I possibly be going now?*

Then, suddenly, Mauli shakes Slobodan, "Slobodan, come to my voice!" Slobodan begins moving toward Mauli's voice.

Ding.

Mauli continues, "Slobodan, come to me!"

Slobodan is moving in all sorts of ways trying to get to the other side, "Get me out of here!"

Mauli rapidly responds with, "Focus all of your energy on turning yourself from within yourself, to between you and me."

Slobodan reaches for his sensorium (the spot in our mind that processes all stimulation from within and between our experiences) and begins screaming as he forcefully pulls on it to get out of this drowning state…

when out of nowhere…

Mauli appears in an elevator.

CO-EXIST AS A UNIVERSAL TRIBE

"Mauli! We did it," Slobodan open his arms and pulls Mauli in for a giant hug. Although, they were no longer Giants.

Mauli replied, "Yes, we did, all thanks to you."

Slobodan looks around the elevator for clues, *a map of a human body with 7 floors?* "Mauli, where are we?"

Ding.

Mauli says, "Although we look like our normal selves again our size is relative to this elevator, we are standing in. We have shrunken down to microscopic people and we are going up to the command center of our readers conscious. The spot in their mind that helps them connect to their body, mind, and spirit to align with their internal and external realities.

You have one more important task to do Slobodan. I need you to walk into this room once the elevator door opens to deliver the takeaway message from this journey of ours. Tell them what you learned through your personal observation.

The room will be filled with the readers tribe of directors that oversee their personality, skills, knowledge, experiences, emotions, ideas, and visions of how they would like their life to be fulfilled.

Some of the readers might not fully know what they want in life just yet, and that is perfectly normal, just encourage them to work on knowing themselves from within, so they can thrive between this universal energy like the bird and the bees are doing..."

Mauli looks down to the floor then back up, "Slobodan, I know this might not have been what you expected, but they are the beneficiaries of this study, and they want to hear what you have to say."

Slobodan takes a breath, stands up straight and says, "Straight from the horse's mouth...

Mauli, I just have one question, are you ready to focus on our energies within, and the energies between for the rest of your life, for what it will make of us will transform the very existence of our lives? As we are no longer without, only between as we journey within."

Mauli looks at Slobodan. "Yes, I am ready to focus the rest of my life on energy within, energy between. I was hired by the readers to find The One that was going to help them improve within for all who come across this experiment. My obligation to them does not end after you walk out of this elevator… Slobodan… we are a tribe for as long as they need us. Plus, we are always within energy, between energy. The Queen and the Heron show us that we must build our awareness and take action toward co-existing as a Universal Tribe."

They both go for the fist bump and say, "till the end." Just like a strong partnership knows what to do when they have achieved unity.

Mauli looks at the elevator panel and notices that the seventh floor is next. "Now, get out there Slobodan, and help them become repetitively aware of the resources within, so they can prepare and enjoy their greatest moments still to come."

THRIVE ON OUR JOURNEY BEYOND

Ding, swooooosh.

As the elevator door opens Mauli pushes a button from inside the elevator that activates a voice to announce Slobodan's entrance.

The directors in the command center hear a pleasant voice over the loud speaker saying, "Directly from our study, the only person to pull the lever, a newfound legend whose name literally means 'Freedom My Sweetheart,' the Giant, the Pet, and the One who is here to help us on our peaceful conquest; please help me in welcoming Slobodan Kuuipo!"

[The crowd goes wild in anticipation for what Slobodan has to say]

Slobodan smiles and waves while walking toward the stool with a glass of water. Slobodan scans the front row to look at the nameplates that read the Director of Belief, Director of Decision Making, Director of Behavior, and Director of Sensorium. All of which, have been patiently waiting to hear what will be said.

Slobodan takes a deep breath, gains composure, and begins speaking, "I sure hope you don't mind me talking about the bird and the bee's?"

[The Audience laughs, smirks, contemplates, reflects on past experiences, and fantastical visions]

. . .

After a powerful pause to let the audience settle down Slobodan continues, "Tonight, I'd like to talk about my encounter with a bird and the bees, and how their efforts to sustain us can teach us a lesson as a Universal Tribe."

Slobodan scans the room looking at everyone directly in their eyes, "Does anyone in here know what THRIVE means?"

The Director of Memory who is sitting in the back of the room blurts out, "thrive means to vigorously prosper."

Slobodan looks at the Director of Memory and says, "That is correct! Your study sent Mauli and me, on a journey across realities to explore the minds consciousness to see if we can help people who are experiencing stress, anxiety, and depression.

We turned into Giants and began exploring this imaginary world approximately 100 years in the future that appeared to be my… "wonderland."

We met the Heron who told us to harness our energy from within as we are never without only between as we are neither here, nor there. Then we were told to find the Bees who taught us that we must live our lives in ways that align with ourselves at the core of our very existence to spiritually transform toward true sociality.

They lived in a hive so big that we, as Giants, were able to sleep in for the night.

Oh, and we got to slide down this wicked honey slide into a lake of honey that they made from all their efforts to sustain our very existence.

How cool is that?"

The Director of Logic shouts out, "Slobodan please excuse me, but what does this have to do with us?"

Slobodan continues, "Great question Director of Logic. Our experience would have little to no value to your command center unless we brought back some valuable information.

So here is something you all can use to your advantage to help this information stick.

I'd like to reintroduce THRIVE only this time as an acronym that means:

Tribes Help Repetitively Inspire Virtually Everywhere.

Let me say that again;

Tribes
Help
Repetitively
Inspire
Virtually
Everywhere.

Inside this room are some of the world's most powerful and influential aspects to your body, mind, spirit, and frankly, the universe. You can use this message to work with one another to THRIVE through your spiritual transformation. Which, we are always on whether you realize it or not.

The point I am trying to make is this: You are like the Queen. Energy within is your command center: the 'body, mind, and spirit' consists of ushers, warriors, and working bees full of energy who are willing and able to help with the experience you command. Only in our case the bees are different forms of energy that take shape to fulfill our needs.

Energy between is an attempt to synergize the connections we make with the world around us in every moment as we move from one measurement of time to the next. Therefore, we are never without for we are connections away from achieving what we desire most.

We can gain more energy when utilizing "energy within, energy between," because the forces at play will begin to work for us rather than against us. Ultimately, decreasing our stress, anxiety, and depression as we move closer to sustainability. Furthermore, with this energy wields great abilities to help make our wildest dreams come true.

I need everyone in this command center to

LOOK AT ME

when I say, "In and of yourself, you are a tribe that can transform and align all your energies with your interests to increase any, and all chances of being happy, grateful, and loving along this path we humans call life."

[Slobodan pauses and basks in this moment where all the directors scan the room looking at one another]

Slobodan smiles. "My highness, you have the potential to single-handedly create a life so vast that any productive effort you put in will enrich your world within the decade. While positively strengthening the Universal Tribe for generations to come."

Slobodan pauses to take a drink out of the glass of water while looking at everyone in the room, and when ready says, "THRIVE will help every particle of energy that embraces this acronym to develop solutions to cope with and endure through all sorts of pain and suffering as we strive to make our world a sustainable place to live.

We are no longer without, everything we need is within and between this moment and the future moments to come. We must figure out what we want so we can connect and align the resources between each other. All said, I encourage every part of you, to explore, learn, and understand the very nature of your core while helping other entities do the same. To understand who you are at the core will make a world of difference as you'll begin to inspire others to make the connection between their spiritual transformations, so they can also THRIVE in a way that works for them.

For the only limitations we have as humans are the ones that we place on ourselves. People from across the planet are suffering; which lead to anger, anxiety, depression, envy, fear, greed, hate, jealousy, stress, and ultimately living with this "without and victim" mindsets that stunt their growth. Not to mention, sufferers are inspiring their behavior in a way that happens to be detrimental to environments virtually everywhere they visit. Therefore, we must enrich our attitudes and choose to THRIVE on our journey's within to move beyond our own limitations.

Out of roughly 7.5 billion people on planet earth. You are our only hope. The world needs you to lead your command center to the best of your ability and to learn from mistakes to THRIVE faster.

Remember that the bees help sustain us as they show us more than anything how much of an impact we can have on our world when we work together by connecting and aligning around our true purpose. Making each one of us a strong member of the Universal Tribe of tribes we are a part of.

If we are going to vigorously prosper, we need to figure out how to follow our heart and mind, and let others follow theirs. Co-exist if you will from the very core of our command centers; like the bees we to can THRIVE within our hive to sustain and help all the other living energies between the Universe.

[Slobodan takes a turn to look out of your eyes, and quickly turns back to continue.]

We must do everything in our power to nurture nature with the command centers that we have, as nature is all we are.

Ultimately, this is our spiritual transformation toward true sociality. Where the bees make honey by pollinating plants, we make dreams come true by thriving with each other and nurturing our kids' abilities to do the same. Follow our hearts and minds, so we can keep the ever-sustaining cycle going for our great, great, great grand kids.

You are enough, and your dreams that come true will help the Universal Tribe thrive on our journey within.

[Slobodan's voice begins to fade into silence as the image fades to black]

Never forget my royal highness, when we become giants, we gain the power to THRIVE; to create, encourage, learn, preserve, share, teach and transform…"

The End

=+=+=

To Growth,

Jeremy Reddig

Lover of The Mind

Email: j@jeremyreddig.com

Website: JeremyReddig.com